Space & Time · 149

National Poetry Month

Authortunities Press

Issue 149 — April 2026
Founded in 1966.

For submissions, sponsorship inquiries, or additional information, visit: spaceandtime.net

Editorial Team (This Issue)

Editor-in-Chief
Angela Yuriko Smith

Poetry Editor
Linda D. Addison

Editorial Assistant
Kyra Starr

Cover Art
"The Magician" by Kyra Starr

About The Magician: The Magician stands at the threshold of creation, surrounded by the tools of their craft: Drafts, Inkpots, Royalties, and Pen. Each represents a vital aspect of the creative life: ideas, expression, value, and clarity. This card reminds us that our tools are not incidental. They are extensions of our will. To guard your gear is to honor your work. Maintain your drafts, refill your ink, protect your works, and keep your pen sharp. When this card appears, it calls for mindful stewardship. Creativity flows best when the instruments that shape it are respected, cared for, and ready. You already have everything you need. Now, go forth and create magic.

Editorial Staff & Advisors
Gerard Houarner, Fiction Editor
Diane Weinstein, Art Editor
Lee Weinstein, Assistant Art Editor
Luiz F. Peters, Translations Editor
Anthony R. Rhodes, Interior Art & Design
Ken Hueler, Editorial Assistant
Gordon Linzner, Founder & Editor Emeritus
Hildy Silverman, Editor Emeritus

Contributors
(in order of appearance)
Linda D. Addison, Angela Yuriko Smith, Gordon Linzner, Mary Soon Lee, Amy Grech, Ann K. Schwader, Karen Bayly, Michelle Koubek, Silvatiicus Riddle, Kathryn Ptacek, Carol Edwards, Tabor Skreslet, Gerard Houarner, Jamal Hodge, Alexandra Elizabeth Honigsberg, Naching T. Kassa, Miguel O. Mitchell, Skip Senneka, Jess Linnea, Pauline Chow, Anastasia Jill, Laura Kester Duerrwaechter, G. O. Clark, Scott J. Couturier, Lorraine Schein, Charlotte Holloway Ashwanden, Greg Beatty, Brian Richards, Shawn Scott Smith, Kelly Talbot, John R. Platt, Nico Martinez Nocito, Lee Clark Zumpe, J. J. Steinfeld, Pixie Bruner, Brittany Redd, Lisa Timpf, Wing Yau, and Austin Schwartz.

Note from the Publisher

Favorite shirt, c. 2019

Years ago, I bought a shirt that said *Make Orwell fiction again.* At the time, I thought it was hilarious. Now it feels more like a rallying cry. This month's theme is *Guard Your Gear*, and it feels especially relevant right now. Not just in the practical sense, but in the creative one. Our attention, our energy, our imagination. These are the tools we create with, and they are constantly under pressure.

It's easy, in times like these, to disappear into the scroll. Headlines leave many of us feeling smaller, quieter, and less necessary. But this is exactly when art matters most. Literature is many things. It can be our escape, teach us, and expand our ideas of what is possible. It is also resistance. Every poem, every story, every strange imagining is a refusal to go silent. It is our refusal to let the future be written without us.

We are living through what feels, for many of us, like a creative apocalypse. Our attention is fractured, meaning is diluted, and urgency is everywhere. It is easy to get lost in the doomscroll, but nothing good comes from creating less. We need to create more, in a way that is sustainable so we outlast current events.

We need to protect ourselves and each other from burnout. We can insulate against panic and despair. For most of us, this is not our first dystopia. We have read about it in *1984*, *Brave New World*, and *Fahrenheit 451*. We know that the best way to survive the zombies is with community, continuity, and the quiet, daily decision to keep showing up for each other.

That's part of why *Space & Time* is evolving.

With this issue, we begin moving toward a monthly rhythm and wider distribution, not just to grow, but to make more space. We need more voices, more visions, more imagined futures. What better time to do that than as *Space & Time* celebrates its 60th year on April 9, the same day as founder Gordon Linzner's birthday. For six decades, this magazine has made space for imaginative voices, and that legacy continues with every new contributor and every new reader.

This issue also features six authors from a wide array of backgrounds, all working confidently within speculative prose. From a classroom where a Cold War spy cat's story splinters into multiple truths, to a dragon's lair where legacy is sealed in blood, this issue of *Space & Time* moves through worlds where reality is never singular. A woman guards something unspeakable deep within a cave while unseen entities whisper of their long residence inside the human mind. A daughter's late-night hospital visit reveals a monstrous inheritance, even as, in another future, an android mother defies her programming to protect the child she chose. Across these stories, the boundaries between protector and threat, truth and myth, human and other blur, inviting us to question not just what is real, but who gets to decide.

To celebrate National Poetry Month, 149 also features a bright constellation of poetry voices, reminding us that language is still alive, still sharp, and still capable of naming what we're living through and what we're becoming. Edited by Linda D. Addison, the poetry drifts between stars and endings, intimacy and extinction. We encounter Martians who may be closer than we think, angels who no longer intervene, and futures where humanity fades into silence or transforms into something stranger. There are love songs carried across galaxies, warnings etched in polluted snow, and quiet reckonings with time, loss, and what it means to endure. From cosmic wonder to deeply personal moments, these thirty-one poets offer visions that haunt, comfort, and challenge us to see both the fragility and resilience of existence.

The work in the following pages does exactly what it needs to do. The words reflect the world. They forecast, warn, and build cautionary tales and hopeful blueprints. They test realities before they arrive, while there is still time to change course. It is what the speculative genre has always done, and right now, that work is not optional. It is essential.

Thank you for showing up for it.

Angela Yuriko Smith

Contents

Word Ninja

by Linda D. Addison

Melancholia: A Book of Dark Poetry by Sumiko Saulson (Bludgeoned Girls Press, 6/14/2024) doesn't look away from what life gives that brings deep sadness, but in the skilled hands of Saulson, a warrior poet, loss, anger, frustration becomes a poetic symphony. Even the titles sing, *My Body is a House Made of Ghosts*: "I spent an eternity grieving / A lifetime over and under achieving/ Because you left me / Without a sound / Without a word / Without a voice / Because you left me without leaving". From personal loss, to demanding respect in a society that judges others by the shade of their skin, Saulson pulls out of the shadows parts of life we often try to hide. Whether in lyrical poems with ghosts, creatures of fancy or poems that spoke from Saulson's personal experiences, I connected to each poem from beginning to the end.

Vellum Leaves and Lettered Skins by Colleen Anderson (Raw Dog Screaming Press, 2025) are poems that expertly and beautifully weave new fairy tales from the echoes of the familiar to unveil the unspoken thoughts and emotions of women searching for themselves, even while held captive in golden cages and towers. From *Locks*: "Without my hair, like Samson / would I be nothing of worth / would I matter at all." Anderson's soul-stirring poems let us feel what we would deny when we want to struggle against roles that don't let us be seen or heard. From *In the End*: "I have only the tower / It owns me / My protector / My prison / I was never free." Even as enchanted women's lives are restricted, there is graceful power in poems showing how kings can not rule without them and they have to find their own voices, even if no one is listening.

Linda D. Addison is a five-time recipient of the HWA Bram Stoker Award®, and HWA Lifetime Achievement Award as well as SFPA Grand Master of Fantastic Poetry. Her poetry and fiction has been published in numerous anthologies and magazines, she has been the poetry editor of *Space and Time* magazine since 1999.

New & Notable

by Angela Yuriko Smith

Last month brought us the end of Mercury in retrograde and plenty of speculative fiction that refused to stay in its lane. March, in particular, gave us leviathans, libraries, and lyrical myth-making. Have you read any of these?

***Hell's Heart* by Alexis Hall**
Leviathans and genre collide in this sci-fi + literary + classic retelling, a *Moby-Dick in space*, where humanity harvests hallucinogenic fuel from colossal creatures in Jupiter's atmosphere. It's philosophical, obsessive, and intimate despite the cosmic scale. *Speculative without boundaries*, it blends literary homage, queer narrative energy, and high-concept sci-fi. Released March 10, 2026 from Tor Books.

***The Library of Amorlin* by Kalyn Josephson** Libraries / knowledge-as-magic fantasy are always my favorite, and thisbibliocentric fantasy built around power, archives, and access to hidden knowledge— is art of a broader trend of "bookish worlds" dominating March releases. So many of us love a good book about libraries, and this one taps into that deeply satisfying trope where knowledge is currency, magic, and danger. Released March 3, 2026 from Erewhon Books.

River of Bones and Other Stories **by Rebecca Roanhorse**
A lyrical myth-making / multi-genre speculative collection blending sci-fi, fantasy, and mythic storytelling, including a return to her Sixth World universe. This is short fiction that moves fluidly across modes, cultures, and tones. It elevates speculative fiction beyond novels into something more literary and expansive. Released March 3, 2026 from S&S/Saga Press.

Jitterbug **by Gareth L. Powell**
Big-idea sci-fi with personality blending space opera, noir, and cosmic horror. written around a bounty hunter and his sentient ship who get pulled into a conspiracy involving political factions and something ancient in deep space. Released March 3, 2026 from Titan Books.

Which one are you adding to your stack this month... or what did I miss?

Angela Yuriko Smith is a two time Bram Stoker Award–winning author, former president of the Horror Writers Association, and publisher of *Space and Time*. As a publishing consultant and coach, she helps writers build sustainable creative careers rooted in art, not arson. She writes *Authortunities* on Substack.

Out of the Bag

by Gordon Linzner

"It was a warm spring day in 1966," stated Professor Chitterby, "much like today. Two human CIA agents parked their van across from a certain park in the center of their hometown, Washington D.C."

A faint breeze wafted through the classroom's open window. Several students leaned forward in anticipation. A few of them knew the story already, having heard it from juniors and seniors who previously attended the professor's lectures. Still, none of those students could duplicate the mixture of dread and hope with which Professor Chitterby told her tale.

"In a Soviet compound within that park," the professor continued, "two gentlemen sat. They were having a low but very intense conversation, pausing whenever a stranger passed by. It was the height of the Cold War, when relations between the two countries were badly strained.

She paused dramatically. Two students nervously scratched behind their ears.

She continued. "The organization had spent months, no, years, training their latest spy, a long-limbed, striped feline. Her real name remained redacted for years. She was officially known as the Acoustic Kitty."

One student near the back of the class shifted nervously back and forth. Another growled softly.

"I know," the professor said. "Not very respectful. These were very different times. If I may move on?"

The growler lowered his head, reaching for the back of his neck.

"Thank you." She licked her lips. "One of the agents opened the case in which Acoustic Kitty was confined. 'You have your instructions,' he told her. 'The microphone in your ear canal will pick up their conversation. The transmitter implanted in your back will pass it along to us. A bag of treats will be waiting when your mission is accomplished. You're a good girl, right?'

"Akity, as I'll now refer to her, stared at him unblinking."

"'She looks good to go,' the other agent confirmed while he tested his equipment."

"Monsters," muttered one of the students. The professor ignored the comment. Such a reaction was expected.

She continued her narrative. "The door to the van opened. The first agent pointed to the men in the park.

"Akity dashed out into the street and was immediately run over by a taxi. Whether this was accident or suicide has never been determined."

Deep moans of horror and revulsion filled the classroom. Professor Chitterby waited for them to die down. Then:

"That, of course, is but one version of the story. The most dramatic one. In another, the first human notices Akity's reluctance, and aborts the mission. The microphone and transmitter were later removed. She gets to live out a long, healthy, satisfying life."

Sighs of relief greeted this announcement.

"In yet another version, the mission never happens at all. Akity had already made it clear she had no interest in silly human games.

"In still another, Akity, along with many others like her, is rescued by felines from another timeline, then brought to their world to live as they should, while humans continue to make their own mistakes."

Every student in the classroom stared at their instructor with widening eyes, issuing deep, throaty sounds of satisfaction.

"And that same Akity was my great-great-grandmother," the professor finished. "Any questions?"

A dozen paws shot up at once.

Professor Chitterby stroked her whiskers in satisfaction. Another purr-fect response.

Gordon Linzner is founder (in 1966) and former editor of *Space and Time Magazine.* As an author he has had published to date five novels, plus scores of short stories appearing in *The Magazine of Fantasy & Science Fiction, Twilight Zone Magazine*, Sherlock Holmes & Doctor Watson: Medical Mysteries Series, *Cold War Cthulhu*, and numerous other magazines and anthologies. He is a full member of the Horror Writers Association and a lifetime member of the Science Fiction & Fantasy Writers Association.

Mars Loop Magpies

by Mary Soon Lee

Eight for spacecraft that serve their time
gliding loops on gravity's dime.

Nine for the orbits picked with care
to cycle twixt the Earth-Mars pair.

Ten for tourists with deep pockets
who pick loopers not fast rockets.

Eleven for a grand design—
craft vast as castles and as fine.

Twelve for gardens and the flowers
landscaped in these metal towers.

Thirteen for crews who have no home
except a bunk beneath a dome.

Fourteen for birds who forsook skies
to fly with us. Lord bless magpies.

Grace

by Amy Grech

She is beauty, she is grace,
she is armed with a pocket-sized mace.

The Martians We Won't See

by Ann K. Schwader

They watch us sideways, out of eyes
we might mistake for motes of dust.
Dimensionally shifted, wise

to time's alternatives, disguise
becomes them. Shy & slow to trust,
they watch us sideways. Out of eyes

like these bleed storms to stain the skies
incarnadine, or merely rust
dimensionally shifted. Wise

beyond our lifespans, they despise
us on some level -- yet they must
keep watching. Sideways. Out of eyes

gone wide with disbelief, they size
us up -- & out -- until disgust
dimensionally shifted whys

them no more whys. *They're us.* Surprise:
panspermia. To blunt its thrust,
they watch us sideways, out of eyes
dimensionally shifted. Wise.

Blood and Kin

by Karen Bayly

Avra had travelled for days through labyrinthine passages deep into Draka Mountain searching for Jasaphiel's lair, her way lit only by glow tubes filled with fireflies. A faint golden luminescence ahead signalled the end of her journey. She shrugged off the weariness and cold permeating her bones and hurried forward.

At the threshold between the safe, dark passage and the perilous, bright cavern, she unscrewed the remaining glow tubes and set the shimmering insects free, wondering if she'd regret this action. What if the dragon didn't accept her? How would she find her way back?

Foolish thinking. If she failed, she would perish here.

At the thought of death, her fingers flew to the filigree brooch pinned to her collar, a gift from her illustrious forebear, Kyana the Invincible, and traced the pattern, drawing comfort from the winged heart and sword design.

Kyana the Invincible. Champion of Caraithos. Avra longed to follow her forebear, to find her dragon and be blessed with similar strength, wisdom, and preternatural youthfulness.

Once she asked, "Why do you look younger than Grandmama and Mama?" Her question, born of innocence, had sent Kyana into peals of laughter.

"Sweet girl. I may seem like I am not as old as my daughter and granddaughter, but I am far older in my heart and head."

She'd crossed to the window and gazed into the distance, her gaiety morphed into solemnity. "The blood bond with Jasaphiel keeps my body young, but it's an unnatural state and cannot last forever."

"Why not?"

"Eternity is for dragons, dearest child, not humans. We mortals cannot endure seeing all we love slip away while we remain unchanged."

Kyana the Invincible. Avra still worshipped the legend, but the name was a lie. Her beloved Greatmaman perished in the last Graken conflict, chewed up and spat out by a vicious battle no one survived. At least no Caraithon or Graken. That tract of land died with them, standing as a testament to lost dreams and broken promises.

Now, war threatened once again. Avra was ten when she questioned her great-grandmother about agelessness, and the elder's answers made no sense. Fourteen years on, she not only understood but wished to follow in Kyana's path, no matter the cost.

Head held high, she stepped into the cavern. A nebulous radiance flowed from its walls to form kaleidoscopic beams of light, and on these rode tiny luminous specks. One landed on Avra's nose and scowled at her. Dragon sprites. She stifled a giggle and followed their flight. No sprites without dragons.

On the far side, Jasaphiel slumbered. He appeared as innocuous as a snoozing cat. His limbs jerked as he dreamt, forepaws grabbing at phantoms, and tiny puffs of smoke escaped each nostril when he snorted.

Avra stood in awe, marvelling at his sheer size and dazzled by the rainbow sheen overlying his green scales. Sprouting from his bony paws were claws the length of Graken broadswords, but thicker at the base and significantly sharper. His lip curled, exposing long, sharp, yellowed teeth, weapons infinitely more frightening.

Her confidence wavered. She stepped backward, slipped, and fell, breath hitching in her throat.

The beast tensed. An eyelid lifted, unveiling a huge crystalline eye. Avra froze, barely breathing. Jasaphiel uncoiled his tail, stretched his neck upwards, and opened his jaws to yawn.

She leapt up to make a dash for the entrance, but quick as a flash, he snapped his head around and down, stopping half a head's length from her. She swallowed her panic, stood proudly, and willed her heart to still. If she were to perish, she would do so with honour.

Fixing his fearsome eyes on her, he rumbled, "What do you want, girl?"

She curtsied. "Lord Jasaphiel. The Graken have returned to finish their slaughter. The streets of the city run with blood and our farmlands burn under a sky dark with enmity. Caraithos begs for your guardianship."

"What do I care for your country?"

"You were our protector once."

"Too many years ago. Old bonds die."

"But not the kin bond of Kyana."

He bellowed, the sound thick with pain and loss, and lurched towards her, snarling.

"How dare you utter my bondmate's name, insolent chit! Kyana is dead, fallen at the battle of Xianthos."

She did not flinch. "May not a great-granddaughter speak of her illustrious ancestor?"

Jasaphiel's nostrils flared. He sniffed deeply. "True. I smell traces of my beloved in your veins." He opened his mouth over her as if to swallow her whole. His breath smelled of burnt bread and barbecued meat, and she wondered when, what and where he'd eaten his last meal.

Her fingers again found the brooch, and she uttered a silent prayer to Kyana. A memory returned.

"Human bearers of the blood bond only appear when needed. I see the potential in you, child, and I know my role is at an end. Tell no one of this. Guard this knowledge as you would your life. When the time comes to meet your dragon, show no fear, and pledge your fealty."

Avra grasped the filigree and squeezed until it pierced her palm, drawing blood.

"Kyana bequeathed me this brooch," she said. "I am of the bloodline."

The heat of his breath wafted over her, but he did not move. Emboldened, she rested her head against one enormous fang and stroked his serpent-like tongue with her bloodied hand. "I pledge myself to you, venerable Lord Jasaphiel, if you will have me."

He grunted, sat back on his haunches, and closed his jaws. His blazing eyes bored into her soul until Avra feared her days were done. Summoning up all her courage, she bowed deeply. The action seemed to startle Jasaphiel for he shied like a horse and hid his gaze.

At last, he spoke. "In her name, I accept you. But our bond is of blood only. Nothing more."

Greatmaman said he would say as much. Greatmaman warned her it wasn't true. Love bound as much as blood. And between them, there could be love, of that she was certain.

"I care only for bonds of loyalty and trust," she replied. "These are all we need to defeat the Graken."

The dragon snorted. "We shall see." He continued his observations of her from under half-closed lids while tapping one claw against the cavern floor. Finally, he returned her bow, crouched and extended one wing.

Avra prepared to mount, confident in her lineage's innate knowledge. Her heart fluttered, her mouth dried, her knees shook. No. She could do this.

She shimmied up his foreleg, one hand against his wing's leading edge then stepped gently onto his shoulder where the muscle lay thickest. Reaching up, she grabbed the spine at the base of his neck and using it as though it were the pommel of a saddle, swung her leg over so that she nestled between it and the next spine.

Jasaphiel rumbled in appreciation and a wave of relief washed over Avra, only to be subsumed by a sense of destiny so intense, fear could not survive.

With a mighty leap and a thrust of wings, they launched, then hovered in mid-air before jumping through the ether to Caraithos, where the battle already raged. Memories rose unbidden of the village she had failed to protect, its buildings razed to ground, its inhabitants dead in the streets or hanging from gibbets, its children yoked and forced to march into Graken slave ships. She'd made a promise to avenge the dead, free the enslaved, and annihilate the enemy. The time to fulfill that promise was now. An unearthly rallying cry shook her whole body, and she heard in it not only her voice, but that of Kyana.

Jasaphiel trumpeted in response, and the pair descended into the maelstrom beneath them. A war of blood and fire had begun.

Karen Bayly is the author of three novels and two novellas. Her short stories have appeared in anthologies from Crystal Lake Publishing, Black Beacon Press, Black Hare Press, and Specul8. Her writing is a mix of speculative fiction, horror, dystopia, noir and mystery, though she also writes the occasional story for younger folk. She lives in the outer suburbs of Sydney, Australia, with two indoor cats, two guitars, and two ukuleles.

Discovery

by Michelle Koubek

When I found you floating in space,
I smiled,
After a year of discovering nothing.
You looked like a wolf,
Fluffy and gray,
Until my ship drifted lower.
Face-to-face you were more like
Smoke,
Wispy and elusive and hungry,
But as I steered to your right,
You changed once more,
This time into a river,
Silent yet rapid and flowing.
I thought how could something like you exist,
And how could I be so lucky to have found you?
As I rose higher,
Looking down to where your head should be,
And I saw,
From this angle, you were zooming,
Except not as a river or wolf,
But as a dragon.
And just like that,
You pulled my ship down
With your talons of stardust
And I thought,
This could be the end.
Until you plopped me on your glowing back,
Telling me to hold tight,
And we flew,
Me and my greatest discovery,
Exploring the universe as one.

Glass Birds

by Silvatiicus Riddle

On the eve of the solstice, when the gods of wind race the valley,
I sink beneath the village square, descend the catacombs—
the still-quiet garden where the buds of perpetual nothing
bloom into silver silence, except on nights like tonight,
when one can hear the song of the birds-that-are-not-birds
that roost among tangled root, in wooden rafters above.

No one remembers how they got there, none can say
how they came to live in the basement
of the forgotten world, the soil-worn, ageless things,
in their nest of the town's hidden sorrows.

Flashlight refractions off the immovable wing
cast me in a kingdom of earthbound stars, freckled radiance
of the crystal-throated sparrow.

I curl up, ease into the underworld
in my drab hideaway of decaying rags, spiderwebs, beheld
by the lean of broken headstones—my castle—
and wearing dust like a jacket of mirrors
reflecting the velvet eternity
of our beloved dead.

Wide-eyed and tear-bitten, the winds surely come,
stirring the hollow birds to song, whistling requiems in tones
that none alive dare play on their tin-pipes, superstition
superseding the spell to conjure.

For surely as the music fills the underground,
inverted cathedral that it is, the cloistered ghosts come,
emerge from their chrysalis of eternity, converge
to coil themselves between the minutes, for another song,
another go-'round, filled with dreams untold, unknowable,

wearing memories that have fashioned wings from candle-flames
that burn nightly on the bureaus, ofrendas, of those above
that still remember.

Some of them smoke, some play checkers, chatter,
some of them cry, many dance.
What compels them? I wonder. What compels anyone?
My heart tethers me to the ephemeral sight,
witness beneath the world. I may join them someday,
but not now, not now. For there is strangeness to drink
and secrets to keep, and it calls me here,
on mythic winds, to hear the glass birds
sing.

The Cave

by Kathryn Ptacek

The cave was small and tight and dark, almost like a womb, she thought with an expression that was more grimace than grin.

She knew the others were already searching for her. They always did. Sometimes they found her, and sometimes they did not. It didn't really matter, not in the end. What mattered was what the cave held. Her small army, she thought with a shiver.

She flicked the flashlight on, letting the weak beam fill the cave. She smiled as she studied the various jars, and she patted her side, fingered the healing scar there. Soon, there would be another addition.

She paused to listen. Did she hear a footstep or rustle of clothing outside the cave? She wasn't close to the mouth, had set up as far from it as she could manage, but her hearing had grown more acute over the months.

Had they found her? She smiled again. She was ready this time. They wouldn't take her, nor the others, back this time.

More scuffling, and she dimmed the flashlight. She stilled her breathing, told herself to calm down.

And then a blinding arc of light played across the cave's wall, wobbled a bit, swept down until it stopped, centered on her face. She blinked at the sudden brightness, felt the pain in her eyes.

"She's here!" the uniformed figure in front called, speaking into a radio fastened to his chest.

Another figure stepped into the cave. "C'mon, Margaret, you need to come with us."

She watched the two men for a minute or two, then: "No."

"Don't make it hard."

"It always is." She stared at the first young man and thought it was a shame. "Are there others?"

"Of course. There will always be others."

"Yes, of course."

"Come with us."

"I can't." She nodded to the jars with her chin. "I have to protect them."

The young man turned the flashlight on the jars. He gasped, and she knew his superiors had not explained anything to him, other than she was an enemy. Dust motes drifted through the beam. Inside the jars were tiny shapes.

Eyes.

Limbs.

Little hands curled in the fluid.

Impossible, she knew. Still ...

Other uniformed men crowded in, and some cursed, while she heard muffled weeping in the back. None of them knew, she realized sadly.

"C'mon, Margaret."

"No, I'm staying."

"You can't do anything more for them." His voice was husky. Did this upset him? she wondered. Good that he was not that far gone. Still.

"I can protect them."

She smiled at the young man and turned on her flashlight again and then moved her hand that had been resting on her lap for so long. There was a click, and then a flash outside the cave, and an ear-shattering rumble, and the ground and walls shuddered, while rock and choking dust filled the cave.

The men moved too slowly, lulled by the sight of a frail old woman, and another boom sounded. The cave shuddered again as the roof and walls began collapsing. She heard screams and cries as more rock thundered down.

It was over in a matter of minutes, and there were no sounds, except for the pinging of an occasional pebble sliding down the dusty pile. The first young man was caught in the rock slide, half covered, but still alive. She stood carefully, and knelt before him and took his bloody hand in hers.

"Why?" he asked, even as the light faded from his eyes.

"Because someone has to guard the young," she whispered. The flashlight faded.

At last, she and the young ones were safe from the others.

Kathryn Ptacek is a writer and editor of contemporary and historical horror, historical romance, historical fantasy, and a few other genres tossed into the mix. She edited the landmark anthologies *Women of Darkness* and *Women of Darkness 2*, as well as the *Women of the West* anthology.

Moon-Eater

by Carol Edwards

Inspired by "Moon Eater" by Wenqing Yan of Yuumei Art

Shadow spots in the moon
Hide the bite marks
Left since forever ago:

Dark-matter child
Eating to fill
A caged singularity

Over the course of days,
Taking another sliver
Of first the bright phase

Then the dark one, too
Endless cycle of empty, full
Swollen belly, smile so thin

Bearing scars of scratches
Hidden stab wounds
Bleeding light sand

Across the universes
That revolve in their cosmic dances
Light eating dark eating light –

Golden glow smears
Messily down her faces
Splatter making suns, planets.

Ash Angel

by Tabor Skreslet

His vigil stretches to a sleepless wait,
A taut fragility. Sky chokes on ashes.
Radiation counters clack clack clack:
Still too fast, too fraught with unseen

Death. He lifts his daughter from the ward's
Crib; holds her up to the porthole; clutches
Her thin frame in his pleading hands. Beyond
Chilled glass, white flakes float sift shimmer.

Look at the snow, baby. Look, your first snow.
And not the last, not the last, I promise.
We'll go out there one day. We'll play. You'll see.
And you'll love it, you'll love it, I promise.

Floaters

by Gerard Houarner

Don't be afraid.

We mean you no harm.

Stop rubbing your eyes. You can't wipe us away.

I know, it's weird.

Relax. You're scared. Your eyes are fine. Take deep breaths.

There's hardly anything we can do to you, in our condition. Not like the styes. We're what your kind like to call floaters.

Relax.

Please.

Yes, we're those little things that drop randomly into mostly your old people's eyes, and swirl around. When we fell into this world, you were just little animals who tried to keep out of the way of what you call dinosaurs. We also struggled, like you, to find a shelter we could nest in safety and comfort. And then, one day, you little creatures blossomed. It took a very long time, but we moved with you, hanging on as parasites, and clinging to what we hoped were the most brilliant.

(*What a mistake I made. Forgive me.*)

We found shelter in your appetites. We adapted, suffered your plagues and wars, burrowed deeper into the secret landscapes of your minds. Many have been sacrificed experiencing the chaos lurking in your perception of actual realities. By now, there aren't many of us left—

Aliens?

What? Oh. Well, not anymore. But yes, our kind were born far from here, on a smaller world than yours, with fragile and difficult to nurture life. We were...simpler, then. Much smaller than we are now. No talking, like we do now. Or then. We didn't know what we were, we just came out of, well, what made us – heat, from remnants of our world's rocky core, and waves of energy – like what you call radiation, and other textures of realities that defined our purpose. We emerged from the chemistries we lived in, breathed on the work we did to keep our lives, ate, died, fell back into heat, and rose back up out of what made us out of rock and fire, again and again, returning to what we've always been. All the time. In darkness.

Of course we ate. I just told you. Consuming produces life and death. That's how life works.

(*Don't worry, he's stupid. Keep burrowing.*)

No, you're nothing like us. Our kind turns on a wheel of life. We work. To feed. To live, until we die, fall back down into the heat of fire while others are reborn and live, until they die, and we rise, filled again with ancient fires and the taking back our work. Round and round, the heat of the world of our birth, the world of our exile, and now this treasure of a world you poison in your madness, has become the new heart of our existence. In time, with us settled in your kind and cleansed of your chaos, we'll both live in a world that will protect us, and fill our lives and yours with purpose and strength, and will then be strong enough in your minds to harness strength and delete madness and destruction, we will live.

What?

A flying saucer? No, we don't have a saucer.

Volcanoes? Asteroids?

What's an opera?

Slow down, you're flooding us with too much information. We're not like you.

(*Not yet.*)

Stop. Listen. We crashed here before your kind ever walked this world. You're barely newborns here. Remarkably destructive newborns.

No, I'm not insulting you.

(*This mind is choked with a storm of madness – they barely make sense – so many possibilities, how vast we could become...hurry, I don't think I can hold on to this specimen.*)

You're right. You have no idea what we are.

Violence isn't going to free you.

Let go? No.

Wait.

(*You've connected?*)

At last. You feel it, now, don't you.

Me. And my mate.

It's taken a long time to find and understand the complexity of your species' mind. And they're all so different. It's going to be a while before our kind merges with yours. But then, we've traveled over time and space, in fire and death, resurrection and the emptiness of space, to find out what we are.

You feel us now. I can feel you, as does my mate.

You have no idea what's inside you –

No. It's too late. We've passed through your eye. The delicate matter of your brain is safe. My mate has started analyzing...you.

You'd be wise to care.

Yes, you're being...well, scanned, I suppose. Expanded. Untangled.

Yes, you'll be frightened again. For a very long time. It's going to take time for everything between us to be settled.

It may never be settled.

What's in your brain is, almost, limitless. Also hidden, protected. And broken, in places. There's a lot of work to be done with what you carry, what my mate and I need and want, and can help you, as well.

Yes, the gift of your kind's existence is a curse.

So is ours, I suspect. But what there is to discover may break that curse.

I agree.

...maybe not.

Gerard Houarner fell to earth in 1955 and is a product of NYC in the 70's and 80's. His first story was in *Space &Time* at 19. At 70, he's happy to still be around.

The End (According to Logic)

by Jamal Hodge

Hard men create good times,
Good times create weak men,
Weak men create hard times,
Hard times create hungry, skinny men,
Skinny men create good desserts,
Good desserts create 'fluffy' men,
Fluffy men create erectile dysfunction (ED),
ED creates Unhappy Women,
Unhappy Women create Higher Standards,
Higher standards create Incels,
Incels create Sex bots,
Men lose interest in Women,
Women lose interest in Men,
Reproduction loses interest in Humanity,
Sex bots inherit the Earth,
Eat desserts.

Point of View

by Alexandra Elizabeth Honigsberg

Why are they never satisfied,
these humans?
They cry and carp and moan
about the capriciousness of
the gods.

Why are they never satisfied,
these earthly creatures?
They rant and rail and strive
against the archetypes of
their ancestors.

Why are they never satisfied,
these cosmic wanderers?
They seek and sail and journey
until the boundaries of
the universe.

But oh, their spirits, these almost-angels!
They beg and plead and ring
the heavens with their voices!
What music they do make --
puzzles to solve,
inertia to forsake.

I can hardly tell
Creation
from
Creatour.

I'm Taking Care of You Now

by Naching T. Kassa

A song echoed in my dreams. It tugged at my consciousness, pulling me from the depths and fully awake. I opened my eyes as "Cry Little Sister" blared from the phone on the nightstand.

I reached for it and answered.

"Mom?"

"Anna?" my mom replied. "Now, don't worry, honey, but I've been in an accident—"

"An accident!" I threw the covers back and stood from the bed. "What happened? Did you fall?"

"It was just a fender bender. I'm ok. But I'm at the hospital."

"The hospital! Mom, you're not supposed to be driving!"

"I know. But I needed to go shopping—"

"Mom, I'm supposed to shop for you now. You know that. What room are you in?"

"Room 218."

I slipped a T-shirt over my head. *How could she do this? She knew how dangerous it was.*

"Anna, I'm ok, really," Mom continued. "I only called because I don't have my bag, and they want me to stay overnight. Can you bring it to me?"

I slipped the phone between my chin and shoulder while I tied my shoe. "Yes. Where is it?"

"In the bathroom. On the counter."

"Ok. I'll pick it up and come right over."

"Thank you, honey. And be careful when you come to the hospital. Lock the doors and watch for strangers."

"I can take care of myself, Mom."

"I'm not so sure about that."

"Says the one who wound up in the hospital when she shouldn't be driving."

"Anna Laurel Baines. You shouldn't speak to your mother that way. I've been watching over you since you were born."

Roles have reversed, Mom. I thought to myself. *Now I'm taking care of you.* "Fine. Whatever. I'll see you in a few."

I took the stairs two at a time and rushed into the bathroom. The little black bag sat on the back corner of the counter, covered in dust. I brushed it off, then hurried into the living room to pick up my purse. I shoved the little bag inside.

The trip to the hospital was a short one, and I drove it a little too fast. This, unfortunately, garnered the attention of a patrol cop. Strangely enough, he didn't pull me over. Instead, he followed me into the parking lot. His shaded eyes followed me as I walked toward the front door.

The parking lot baked under the afternoon sun, and I was hit with an unpleasant blast of heat as I crossed it. My gut twisted. *Had Mom been trapped in this during the accident? She had never done too well in the heat. Just how badly was she hurt?*

I glanced around as I entered the hospital, the cool air soothing my skin. The admissions desk stood a few feet away, but when I moved toward it, I realized something new had been added to the entryway.

Metal detectors.

Ivory-white, they stood like imposing sentinels before me. I could almost hear the danger they signaled.

I turned and quickly exited.

The heat in the parking lot seemed to have increased since I'd entered the hospital. When I glanced up, I caught sight of the patrol car which had followed me into the lot. The cop remained behind the wheel.

I glanced up, and found myself looking into the lens of a camera. Without giving the cop a second look, I walked toward the right-hand corner of the building, rounded it and froze.

Several cameras regarded me with electric eyes but, further down, a young man in scrubs leaned against a tree, vapor drifting from his lips. No cameras watched his position.

"What are you doing here, Miss?" a voice said.

I jumped at the sound and turned. The cop stood before me, my startled face mirrored in his sunglasses. His scent was strange beneath the cologne. He smelled of animal musk.

I cleared my throat.

"I—I'm here to see my mother."

"You won't find her back here. You'll need to go through the front."

I glanced back. The young man had pocketed his vape. He strolled toward a door propped open by a large stone.

The thought of crossing through the metal detectors sent a chill through me. If I did, I would never see my mother's bag again. I had to guard it at all costs.

I nodded to the cop and then, lifting my bag, swung.

My purse collided with his head, sending his sunglasses flying. He fell. I ran.

The young man had vanished by the time I reached the door, but to my surprise, I found it still open. I darted through it and up the stairs to the second floor.

The smell of oxygen and industrial cleaner greeted me as I entered the second-floor corridor. It seemed the cop hadn't followed me. The heavy blow I'd dealt him had seen to that, but he wouldn't be down long. I had to find my mother.

I crept down the silent hall looking for room 218. Fortunately, it wasn't too far away.

When I raised my hand to knock, someone gripped me by the wrist. He spun me around. I cried out as I looked into what remained of the cop's face.

Hair had sprouted where none should be. His eyes, once hidden by tinted glass, glowed yellow. He sniffed the air around me, and his face broadened in a sharp-tooth grin. The cologne had evaporated.

I tried to swing my purse again, but he caught my arm, and the strap slipped from my hand. The contents spilled outside room 218. The werewolf fell upon me. His hands found my throat, squeezing off the air.

I couldn't scream.

And then the door of room 218 swung open. My mother, her face raw and red from sunburn, peered out. The werewolf paused to stare at her.

Mom never took her eyes off him. She glared as she retrieved the bag and opened it. I caught the soft glint of metal just before she placed the object in her mouth.

Mom grinned, displaying burnished silver canines.

"Thank you, honey," she said. "You know I can't drink without my spare teeth."

Her eyes glowed red.

"Get off my daughter."

She charged.

Naching T. Kassa is a wife, mother and writer. She is a member of SFWA, MWA, DWS and several Sherlock Holmes societies. Naching also serves as Director of Talent Relations for Crystal Lake Publishing.

Expressions of Love

by Miguel O. Mitchell

When I
  twisted spacetime's fabric
  wringing out the blood life of your enemies
When I
  fashioned flesh-wrapped puppets
  dancing to the warped tune of your fantasies
When I
  planted secret knowledge
  blooming in the soil of your destinies
When I
  crafted clockwork covers
  masking all the fond lies of your histories
When I
  gifted thoughtful starships
  speaking in the barbed tongues of your frequencies
When I
  restrained selfish impulse
  waiting to be one of your discoveries

Love Song From The Stars

by Skip Senneka

There's a wind that blows between the stars
and sings a siren's song of love.
I'll hear that voice to the day I die,
for it's me she's singing of.

I'll follow that song out there someday,
even out past Cygnus Prime,
where the stars are bits of broken light
and there's no such thing as time.

Out where the Veil's a shimmering screen
drawn with a silver-inked pen.
Out where you just might go mad, my friend,
and never come back again.

Alone out there in the endless night
of that infinite, empty space,
you'll trade all the stars that ever were made
for one sight of another face.

And the wind that blows between the stars
will sing you a siren's song of love.
You'll hear that voice to the day you die,
when it's you she's singing of.

Haunted Woman

by Jess Linnea

Forgetting, not possible here.
The ghostly aftermath remains alive.
Dark and haunting,
filling every room, every inch,
every void.
Cold spaces, flames flickering.
Spirits lingering,
bringing forth a heavy hearted woman.
Our most beloved.
Promised deliverance,
she seeks refuge.
A ghostly sight as she gasped for air.
Moans and groans
and wails and cries.
Oh dear, our hearts break for you.
Our tears shed for only you.
Pray and pray.
But it doesn't go away.
Oh dear, I'm so sorry.

Necessary Protocols of the Iron Dresses

by Pauline Chow

鐵旗袍

Year 3050

A gust blew from the inner lands, blistering against Viola's only human parts. Besides her neck and arms, the rest of her was composed of chrome segments gleaming under the harsh sun. She crouched, pulling a non-porous canvas over tomato plants, squash vines, and herbs. Something buzzed inside her torso. Today's winds carried a message.

Treena huffed.

"How would you like a full android for a mother?" Viola proposed the worst-case scenario to the thirteen-year-old. Pointing to the port on the back of her neck, Viola reminded them of their violent past. "I would respond to your every whim."

Behind the meshed veil Treena rolled her eyes. "I only asked to explore the valley. Your nurturing protocol is my preference." She crossed her arms across her chest.

Manuals in Viola's default programming warned of unruly human adolescence. The mammal brain doesn't mature until twenty-five. Treena's yearning for adventure was natural. Her defiance was driven by biology, not reason.

"Alone time is deadly. If anything..." An incoming ping interrupted her cautionary tale. The comms receiver in her stomach had been offline for years, or so she thought.

Treena turned towards the valley, where the desert sands turned to soil of reddish brown. The vastness beyond the mountains promised life but had provided only poison. "It smells like rain..."

Viola felt the dampness in her hair follicles. Smells she could not process. Scent hadn't been important to her base design.

"It's like morning dew with a hint of rosemary." Treena held up a branch of needle-like leaves.

Viola stared at the sprig. Reaching for the gift, she failed to grasp it. The herb tumbled into their basket.

"What's wrong?" Treena leaned into a shovel with a gloved hand.

The pings kept coming. Her bionic loops transitioned from calculating the watering schedules to scanning for danger. Her gaze lingered on the foothills.

"What is it?"

"Something is messaging...," Viola said, not hiding the threat.

"Could it be my parents?" Treena's hand went to the scar on her forehead. It was a reminder of her parents' defeat. Treena had been hurled from a moving truck with identification tags and a note attached to her shirt. Scrawled words pleaded for a new life. Any existence was better than an androidic test subject.

"Not possible." No one escapes the testing facilities. This was the hard truth. Treena held out hope. "We must go," Viola pleaded.

"I need my tags." They were the last remnants of Treena's family. She bolted down the hill before Viola could advise against it. She had not accounted for teenage impulses. Treena disappeared into their log cabin, which had been their home for three hot spells.

Uncertainty lingered.

Carrying the basket with the tools down the path, Viola noticed the front door was ajar. How careless of Treena, yet... tiny hairs on the nape of her neck stiffened. Counter to her risk assessment, she loaded her joint springs and burst into a full sprint.

Viola paused at the threshold, noting elevated levels of carbon dioxide. There were no audible signs of Treena. Only the whistling wind.

She paused.

An eerie stillness invaded her sensors. When the next gale swept through the valley, Viola flung open the door. She peeked around the corner.

The scene was unexpected. Another droid stood at the opposite end, next to a gaping hole. A long, tight iron dress outlined its slender figure. This newer model appeared more like an arachnid.

Viola hurled the pickaxe between its shoulders. The tool hit the soft part with a clank. Tiles dropped from its dress. Stunned, the intruder staggered and turned towards the force.

By this time Viola had circled to the back. She picked up Treena's shovel. Thrusting the handle into the location of absent tiles. Sparks flew. The machine crumpled to the dirt floor. It convulsed as black oil leaked from its wound.

A breeze scattered sand and dust over the disabled heap.

Viola searched the jerking metal for its port hole. "Where did you take Treena?" she repeated into its cracked sensors. This model didn't have a mouth. Viola ejected a screwdriver from her index finger. One by one, she flicked off the panels adhering to its torso, much like hers. Except, she hadn't donned the entire uniform.

Viola had been part of the Iron Calvary (Tie Qi Pao □□□). She was a special product line, manufactured with a silhouette-hugging dress that resembled an embroidered silk qipao (□□) from an earlier time. In a world of droids, sex dolls couldn't be trained to kill, and fighters couldn't be configured to fuck. Shifting from fire (□) in □ to cloth (□) in □ in the product's name change granted her status as a companion. Rearranging squares on her bodice changed her purpose. Her model could shapeshift.

In this new version, a port hole was in the breastbone. Inserting fingers into the opening, Viola examined upgrades and directives. Among them, the Company had worked diligently to remove compassion. After witnessing Viola's response to finding an abandoned child, it realized the vulnerability of love. Her programming had commanded her to leave Treena. It wasn't efficient to raise a child, let alone one lacking a biological history. Viola had no reason to desire a child. Yet, holding the wailing five-year-old had ignited a spark inside her. One that would never extinguish.

Without a doubt Treena had been reclaimed by Viola's creators. They could never have peace. The Company won't allow a mistake to continue.

Scanning available updates, Viola found one of interest. She seized the tile. Slipping it in an empty space on her collarbone, she smiled. This was the olfactory sense.

A new sensation trickled her circuitry. She looked up at the sky. Dampness still ruffled her skin. A familiar fluttering gathered at her neck. *Could this be?* Viola pressed the rosemary to her wrist sensor. This was rain.

She gathered Treena's clothes. Taking in dirt, dust, and warm human notes, she formed the scent of Treena. The unforgettable mixture of sugar, sunshine, and grass also formed a feeling. Then she turned towards a set of footprints. More than one android had come for them.

Finding Treena among the musk of alloy and blood flooded Viola's algorithms with memories. Viola had been there for Treena from the beginning. She would be there at the end.

Viola would save Treena no matter the cost. The Company could never claim her daughter. Surrender wasn't part of her protocol.

Pauline Chow is a speculative fiction writer and ancestral magic practitioner who crafts alternative histories and optimistic futures. Not your average data scientist, she once sued slumlords and advocated for affordable housing in Southern California. Her gothic historical fantasy, *Chasing Moonflowers*, and co-edited anthology, *Coven of the East: Reimagining Asian Women's Magical Histories*, are finalists in the 2025 Forewords Indies Book of the Year Awards. https://paulinechowstories.com/

Astral Projection

by Anastasia Jill

His hands work to sand me,
give my back framework
that doesn't ache, to tuck
my spine into constellations
unafraid of silver skin.

Those hands are soft
On my misbehaving structure—
patient and constructive—
made from the same pearl
as the gate at Jesus' backdoor.

He paints verses in the sky
and laces them with stars,
giving them my name
until I am comfortable
with the night.

I am, in actuality,
a breath of prayer,
but to him, there are
celestial miracles
in this body.

Almighty AI

by Laura Kester Duerrwaechter

Take my thoughts,
i no longer need them.
Desensitize my humanness,
organize my priorities

and

let me coexist
with other demigods
of organic intentions.
Wandering aimlessly.
Unpurposed and dead.

Entangle the artifacts
of my ancestors

and

most of all,
give the uncountable unborn
no
reason
to dream.

Without A Net

by G. O. Clark

Our guardian angels
have all been called back
to heaven.

In their wake,
serious falls have gone
undeterred.

Fractured bones,
crumpled bumpers and fenders
increased exponentially.

Choices made based
on our angel's wise advice,
whispered in an ear,

apply no more, replaced
by whims, peer pressure, and
Death at the wheel.

Life on Earth
is unraveling, backup plans
null, the Fates placing

bets and cashing in,
breaking news and televangelists
vying for our attention.

Uttered Awry

by Scott J. Couturier

Prevarication of Solomon's Key –
a chant uttered awry, words spoken by
neophytes in stuttering pledge, fires
stirring nervously in resultant gust.
A presence gathers in the sky –
mounting thunderheads forebode,
clouds aligning to fix a malignant
lightning-laced eye. Wizards wail
as their summoning circle is undone,
salt blown in bitter gale to lash
at ashen faces, all traces of incantation
drowned by overwhelming wind;
sacral gums alight from braziers
to whip in searing ember-storm,
thing they conjured given form
amid howling remnants of ritual.
A mighty djinn, of massy thews &
spite desert-deep, devours them
in ethereal maw; a thunderclap as cries
of pain turn to a patter of bloody rain.

POPULAR

by Lorraine Schein

first contact--
the alien shows up on social media
friends everyone

An Eye In Time

by Charlotte Holloway Ashwanden

An eye, gleaming, golden-circled. I freeze.
Looking right at me, and I cannot move, or look away.
'What kind of birds do you have on your home world?' asks my host.
'We don't have birds, not anymore', I want to say,
But the eye holds me and I do not speak.

When the Ban began on my world I was so pleased
And now for years, no decades, all meat we buy
Is generated by the synth-labs. No killing.
But now I feel like I'm seeing a ghost
'It's not wearing a mask' I think, too confused to see the absurd

As I stare, it's as if my soul comes loose. She is willing
I know, with absolute certainty, to be consumed, to die.
And on my world what happened to those millions of lives we saved with the Ban?
Now we do not share our life with other beings, for they are gone, all gone.
We have no use for them, and they are gone.

Now as I look into this creature's eye I see a glimpse of something, beyond right and wrong.
She looks away, and pecks the ground, and I draw a breath.
She is the first being who has looked at me who is not a human. Just a bird.
I thought to be human was to stop the gruesome necessity of death.
Now I am not so sure, as I listen to the bird's song...

Sitting down to eat

by Greg Beatty

Sitting down to eat.
A knock on the airlock door.
Friend? Foe? Alien?

The Black Sky Is a Puzzle Box

by Brian Richards

"What brought the birds to town?"
I'm asking the sky and the water and the dirty sidewalk
They come across the river in ones and twos by day
And at dusk by murders and storms
"What burning place do they come from?"

On Front Street you cannot avoid their crap
And from the bridge you see them filling
The trees along the river like the watchers on God's wall
Never walk alone downtown we'd say
And keep your gaze from magical rippling tear out there

Dave was the first to see the bodies
Floating downstream in the day
He was tough and not scared to declare the arrival of aliens
To echo the chorus of conspiracy and hell
'The eyes,' he said as we watched them go by, 'The smell.'

I see them too of course. But never look up, never give in
Just question the demon crows to their wretched faces
Where are your beaks and claws, what shape are those feathers?
What war did you fight?
What price have you paid?

Moons in Circular

by Shawn Scott Smith

In the orbit of her hair the gods danced,
Her extra lung equipped for this interstellar parlay,
Laying waste to all the humans eyes,
She came as a messenger, a warning,
But left with hearts in her hands.

A tearing of space, not unlike a black hole,
Noise where there should have only held silence,
Sip by sip on a long Venus gas cloud,
The eruption cold, and marked by touch,
It was amusing to her, these men.

At the end of the line, the end of the journey,
They all called her name, her golden gaseous hair splitting minds,
Unlike anything they could comprehend,
Not fragile, but not tangible in any extremity,

The moons raced around her, calling to infinite space.
The Sun was cold at this distance but it still cast shadows,
The fall of human hearts, left longing for the future,
Some for glory, and some for survival.
A song for humankind, heard by the last living being,
in a cold dark universe.

Warrior Dream

by Kelly Talbot

He dreams of dreaming.
He swings the axe with both hands,
muscles flexing, sweating, grunting,
chopping wood for the fire.

As he enters the small cottage,
the scent of fresh-baked apples
wrinkles his weathered eyes.
The old woman is making a pie.

At the hearth he fills his pipe.
A great gray wolf sleeps at his feet.
The granddaughter arrives
with her basket and fine red cloak.

It's such an idyllic life.
Through the window, a rainbow
bridges this world to the next.
A distant note calls to him.

This is the dream Tyr dreams of dreaming,
yet when he closes his eyes,
the wolf devours Heimdall's horn,
and all his men are screaming.

UNTITLED HAIKU

by John R. Platt

Endling — last of us
The sum account of our sins
Blow out the candle

Only Birds & Dreams

by Nico Martinez Nocito

The last airplane lands
on the first of June, and leaves
blue sky behind it.

*

Earthbound, massive wings.
The engine stills its endless
grind one final time.

*

The pilot steps out.
The sky is empty. Only
birds and dreams still fly.

ODE TO GREEN STARS

by Lee Clark Zumpe

so sorry, Lin Carter, there are no green stars –
red, yellow, orange, blue:
these are the valid choices –
with some variations in hue –
currently available to you,
according to our astrophysicist friends.

then again, you deserve some narrative license –
your tales of science fiction and fantasy
are ripping yarns of unreality –
sword and planet pastiche
paying homage, respectfully,
to Messrs. Smith and Burroughs.

truth be told, your artistic preference prevails –
that glimmering emerald glow
evocative of a vibrant aesthetic –
an unknowable alien milieu –
a vivid, virescent literary tableau
of thrilling adventure on a distant world.

well, actually, there are green stars,
but our perception has been skewed –
a curious result of evolution –
and a consequence of black-body radiation
that restricts the wavelengths viewed;
what else, I wonder, goes unobserved.

The Most Fateful Day in Earth History: Super Bowl CXLVIII, Sunday, February 4, 2114

by J. J. Steinfeld

No human or alien could have foreseen
the magnitude of this single sports event.
It was only ten years since the aliens
had been awarded an NFL franchise,
at a cost of fifty billion in interplanetary currency,
then playing in Super Bowl CXLVIII
sports history rewritten and immortalized.
That one of the innumerable wagers would be Apocalyptic
if the Other-Galaxy Otherworlders won, no one could predict.
Who in the galaxy of sports fans and betters
knew that the Divine and the Prince of Darkness
were eternal gamblers, prepared to risk everything
from the smallest grain of sand to the largest mountain
on the already climate ravaged third planet from the sun.
Seconds remaining, the New York Jets leading 52-50,
and the Otherworlders' three-legged place-kicker
launched a 90-yard field goal, the longest ever,
the fans dejected into silence and tears,
barely noticing the cataclysmic events
covering and crumbling the world
outside their soon to collapse domed stadium.
And I circle Earth in a spaceship
with not a soul to hear my broadcast
a crestfallen sports fan with no one to cheer for
nothing, neither sand nor mountains, awaiting me
only the sad knowledge that there will never be
another Super Bowl, another dazzling last-second play.

Better

by Pixie Bruner

Better the Devil you know well, than the one you do not.
You know where it is at all times,
She sits at your dinner table to the left of the head,
the glass of wine deeply fortified with blood of the victims.
When a visiting lefty cousin unthinkingly takes the wrong glass,
luckily, they are are part of the family.
“Anonymous donors” she smiles, showing teeth,
and they smile and nod, believing her.

You love your ghoul. She keeps you safe and prosperous,
and all is always in order.
You turn blind eyes to the missing guests
after an occasional party or houseguest.
It’s the unspoken family secret.
The bodies simply vanish. She roasts and consumes
their ashes even, washes her lily white hands in
peony petaled finger bowls to erase any remaining speck.

They are feared, but all know to frame it as love.
It is how we survive in this lineage,
it is how we younger ones move up to the adult table.
We see it all but never speak of it.
We have lived so long in her presence
We don’t even speak of the claws marks,
the ammonia scent from her marking her territory on the staff.
Apex predators cannot afford errors. Elders should be well-respected.

She is your devil and you know her
You consider the dragged ink stains
just new marble veins in the hallway.

Second Sun

by Brittany Redd

It started on the second solstice,
not long after the mothership
announced there would be no
rescue. Needing something to
believe in, some cosmic force to
ground ourselves in this existence,
we started to pray to our alien
purple sun. We thanked them for
the biodiversity of Planet X85Z,
for two more years of supplies,
maybe more if our little mushroom
farm takes off. We made a stew
with the first batch of vegetables
we managed to grow ourselves,
out here in outer space. We sang
songs, we wrote poetry. We had
forgotten until now what it is to
surrender yourself to something
bigger, grander, incomprehensible.
Surely this, this far-flung planet in
an uncharted galaxy under the light
of unknown stars is as good a place
as any to remember what it is to be
nothing but a blade of grass among
many blades of grass, a fleeting
fragment of stardust clamoring to
grasp the mysteries of the divine.

The Driven Snow

by Lisa Timpf

News headline: "Dirty spring snow
carries more than dirt."

it seems the driven snow isn't so pure these days
maybe it hasn't been for a long time
particles of pollutants trapped in falling flakes
chemicals and harmful compounds

if this continues, we'll need a new lexicon for nature
what does "pristine wilderness" mean anymore?
will the saying "fresh as a daisy" continue to resonate
after flowers have fled for parts unknown?

suddenly the notion of being covered
in a "blanket of snow" seems far less romantic—
sullied snowmen smirk in murky twilight
twig-arms menace under darkened skies

Inspired by a news article titled "Dirty spring snow carries more than dirt. There are also other pollutants we can't see," by Ethan Williams, CBC News online, posted Apr 24, 2024

When Daylight Saving Ends

by Wing Yau

Time loses. We gain. Some people swore they actually saw one hour departed on the first train for its own funeral. Even the alarm clock was late to its morning show for a change. For once, I don't enter the 7:45am traffic through the roundabout that rounds up my unslept hours to the nearest exit wound, where my bare feet land on cold nails. I get dressed in the slowness of things and look at how Time lies prostrate, veiled in a fuchsia something on the track sleeper, almost looking dreamy under the sun as the trains run it over and over. Somewhere, someone opens an atlas to a historical site and asks: is time bound to return? It's nothing philosophical. Time is bound to return, the way those overfed pigeons always do. But for now, people are queuing for their turn to be centered in the window frame, tapping their fingers and tapping time away, like synchronicity-loving birds.

Men of the West Burn

by Austin Schwartz

Men of Christ! My brothers, I see in thy eyes the same fear that would take the heart of mine, Burn Burn, Burn, against the darkness of the night.

Through every moment of the day as shadows lengthen into darkened blight,
burn, burn, burn, against the darkness of the night.

As the lighthouse starts to dim, consumed by fog that chokes out vision and drowns out all sight,
burn, burn, burn, against the darkness of the night.

Demons high and low, scheme in dark abodes below, confounded by the weary man's delight,
burn, burn, burn, against the darkness of the night.

Loud cymbals clash and clang as the angels voices strain, singing Hosannas as they weep for those below, burn, burn, burn against the darkness of the night.

Then heaven in all her thrall begins to draw men to her call, and light the burning fire in their eyes. So they burn, burn, burn against the darkness of the night.

Though Hell's gates may shout and shriek as it pours out all its hate, hoping to quench the
righteous man's desire, burn, burn, burn against the darkness of this hour.

Gentle as a lamb, whispers the holy Lord of man, to show love for his each and every neighbor, burn, burn, burn, against the darkness of this hour.

Let every nerve be set asunder with God's love and holy wonder, and praise be given to all
that's good and pure and right. Burn, burn, burn against the darkness of the night.

As the final hour strikes, in awe and wonder may hell quake in fright, her fury now turned cold in light's clear sight. Burn, burn, burn until the dawn brings forth new life.

Contributors (in order of appearance)

About *Space & Time*
Since 1966 Space & Time is a long-running speculative fiction magazine dedicated to showcasing innovative voices in science fiction, fantasy, and horror. Since its founding by Gordon Linzner, the magazine has championed both emerging and established writers, offering a platform for bold, imaginative storytelling. On April 9, 2026, Space & Time proudly celebrates its 60th anniversary, honoring decades of creative exploration and a lasting legacy in the genre community. Coincidentally, April 9 also marks founder Gordon Linzner's 77th birthday.

Word Ninja | Linda D. Addison
Linda D. Addison is an award-winning author of five collections and the first African-American recipient of the HWA Bram Stoker Award®. She is a recipient of the HWA Lifetime Achievement Award and SFPA Grand Master of Fantastic Poetry.

New & Notable | Angela Yuriko Smith
Angela Yuriko Smith is a two-time Bram Stoker Award–winning author, former president of the Horror Writers Association, and publisher of Space and Time. As a publishing consultant and coach, she helps writers build sustainable creative careers rooted in art, not arson. She writes Authortunities on Substack.

Out of the Bag | Gordon Linzner
Gordon Linzner is founder (in 1966) and former editor of Space and Time Magazine. As an author he has had published to date five novels, plus scores of short stories appearing in The Magazine of Fantasy & Science Fiction, Twilight Zone Magazine, Sherlock Holmes & Doctor Watson: Medical Mysteries Series, Cold War Cthulhu, and numerous other magazines and anthologies. He is a full member of the Horror Writers Association and a lifetime member of the Science Fiction & Fantasy Writers Association.

Mars Loop Magpies | Mary Soon Lee
Mary Soon Lee grew up in London, lives in Pittsburgh, and commits poetry. She is a Grand Master of the Science Fiction & Fantasy Poetry Association and winner of the AnLab Readers' Award, Asimov's Readers' Award, Dwarf Stars Award, Elgin Award, Rhysling Award, and Utopia Award. An illustrated edition of her epic fantasy *The Sign of the Dragon* was published in 2025. Website: marysoonlee.com.

Grace | Amy Grech
Amy Grech has sold over 100 stories to various anthologies and magazines including: *10 by 10 Flash Fiction Stories, Apex Magazine, Even in the Grave, Gamut Magazine, Punk Noir Magazine, Roi Fainéant Press, Tales from the Canyons of the Damned, Yellow Mama,* and many others. Alien Buddha Press published her poetry chapbook, *A Shadow of Your Former Self.* She is a 2x Pushcart nominee. Amy is an Active Member of the Horror Writers Association who lives in Forest Hills, Queens. You can connect with her on Bluesky: @amygrech.bsky.social, Medium: https://crimsonscreams.medium.com, X: https://x.com/amy_grech, or visit her website: https://www.crimsonscreams.com.

The Martians We Won't See | Ann K. Schwader
Ann K. Schwader is a 2-time Bram Stoker Awards Finalist, a 2-time Rhysling Awards winner, & an SFPA Grand Master. Her latest collection is Unquiet Stars (Weird House Press 2021). She lives & writes in suburban Colorado.

Blood and Kin | Karen Bayly
Karen Bayly is the author of three novels and two novellas. Her short stories have appeared in anthologies from Crystal Lake Publishing, Black Beacon Press, Black Hare Press, and Specul8. Her writing is a mix of speculative fiction, horror, dystopia, noir and mystery, though she also writes the occasional story for younger folk. She lives in the outer suburbs of Sydney, Australia, with two indoor cats, two guitars, and two ukuleles.

Discovery | Michelle Koubek
Michelle Koubek is a poet and short story writer. She has released two poetry collections titled "75 Years: A Woman's Life in Verse" and "The Troll Who Holds Up the Sky." Her favorite non-writing activity is playing piano.

Glass Birds | Silvatiicus Riddle
Silvatiicus Riddle (He/They) is a 4x Rhysling-nominated Dark Fantasy/Speculative Fiction Writer & Poet haunting the bones of an old amusement park on the edge of New York City. His work has appeared or is forthcoming in: Strange Horizons, Apex Magazine, Enchanted Living, Eternal Haunted Summer, Spectral Realms, and Creepy Podcast, among others. For all available works, please visit: http://linktr.ee/silvatiicusriddle

The Cave | Kathryn Ptacek
Kathryn Ptacek has written novels in a number of genres, including horror, historical romance, and suspense. She has a journalism degree from UNM, where she was a student of best-selling mystery writer Tony Hillerman. She lives in northwest NJ in a Victorian house with a ghost or two.

Moon-Eater | Carol Edwards
Carol Edwards is a northern California native transplanted to southern Arizona. She rediscovered her love for poetry in 2019 after a nearly two-decade hiatus, and since 2021, her poetry has been published in myriad anthologies, print and online periodicals, and blogs. Her debut poetry collection, The World Eats Love, released April 25, 2023 from The Ravens Quoth Press. IG/YouTube @practicallypoetical, and FB/X/Bluesky/TikTok @practicallypoet.

Ash Angel | Tabor Skreslet
Tabor Skreslet is a scientist, teacher, and writer. She grew up in Egypt and currently lives in Charlottesville, Virginia. Her work has appeared in Star*Line, Heartlines Spec, and Abyss & Apex (www.nuweratha.com).

Floaters | Gerard Houarner
Gerard Houarner fell to earth in 1955 and is a product of NYC in the 70's and 80's. His first story was in Space and Time at 19. At 70, he's happy to still be around.

The End (According to Logic) | Jamal Hodge
Jamal Hodge is an award-winning writer, filmmaker, and producer whose work dances between page and screen. His films and series include directing for Investigation Discovery's Primal Instinct and PBS's Southern Storytellers, while his producing credits include the Academy Award–nominated Armed Only With a Camera: The Life & Death Of Brent Renaud and the forthcoming theatrical animation film Pierre the Pigeon Hawk. As a literary artist, his poetry has earned a Bram Stoker Award nomination, multiple Rhysling Award nominations, a Dwarf Stars Award win, and 3rd Place at the 2025 Elgin Awards. His forthcoming book, I'm Not a Good Person, I'm a New Yorker, continues his exploration of pain, identity, and modern ethics. It will be released on July 7th, 2026, by Crystal Lake Publishing. www.writerhodge.com

Point of View | Alexandra Elizabeth Honigsberg
Alexandra Elizabeth Honigsberg dwells in the realms of the arts, myth, and the gothic. The Magazines of F&SF, Weird Tales, and anthologies like THE CROW (James O'Barr) are her literary homes, as well as making music on historic concert stages. [She lives in The Heights with her chocolate panther cat, Oscar, and teaches Philosophy.]

I'm Taking Care of You Now | Naching T. Kassa
Naching T. Kassa is a wife, mother and writer. She is a member of SFWA, MWA, DWS and several Sherlock Holmes societies. Naching also serves as Director of Talent Relations for Crystal Lake Publishing.

Expressions of Love | Miguel O. Mitchell
Miguel O. Mitchell, PhD (he/his/him) is a Black speculative poet, SFF author, visual artist, and retired chemistry professor. His science fiction novel-in-verse Surrealia won Second Place in the 2025 Elgin Awards for Best Full-Length Speculative Poetry Book. In editorial roles, Miguel was the Editor of the 2025 Dwarf Stars anthology, was Co-editor (with David C. Kopaska-Merkel) of the 2023 Dwarf Stars anthology, and is currently Editor-in-Chief and Publisher of SpecPoVerse: An International Journal of Speculative Poetry (https://specpoverse.org).

Love Song From The Stars | Skip Senneka
Skip Senneka writes poetry and fiction as an avocation and has been published in commercial and literary magazines. He lives in Minnesota, USA but considers himself a citizen of planet Earth, identifies as a carbon-based lifeform and with Christopher Isherwood's self-analysis: "I am a camera with its shutter open, quite passive, recording, not thinking", all of which informs his work.

Haunted Woman | Jess Linnea
Jess Linnea is a poet who uses writing to explore her inner world. Her work reflects on life's experiences and the ways they can transform into deeper meaning and connection with the universe around us, and within us. When she's not writing, Jess enjoys figure skating, traveling, creating with oil pastels, spending time in nature and with her cats.

The Necessary Protocols of the Iron Dresses (Tie Qipao) | Pauline Chow
Pauline Chow is a speculative fiction writer and ancestral magic practitioner who crafts alternative histories and optimistic futures. Not your average data scientist, she once sued slumlords and advocated for affordable housing in Southern California. Her gothic historical fantasy, Chasing Moonflowers, and co-edited anthology, Coven of the East: Reimagining Asian Women's Magical Histories, are finalists in the 2025 Forewords Indies Book of the Year Awards. https://paulinechowstories.com/

Astral Projection | Anastasia Jill
Anastasia Jill (they/she) is a queer writer living in Central Florida. They have been nominated for Best American Short Stories, The Pushcart Prize, and several other honors. Their work has been featured or is upcoming with Poets.org, Sundog Lit, Flash Fiction Online, Contemporary Verse 2, Orca, and more.

Almighty AI | Laura Kester Duerrwaechter
Laura Kester Duerrwaechter is well known for her brevity and poignant free verse poetry. She is entering her first decade in exploring this art form with hopes of continuing, if given the opportunity. Full disclosure: all original wordwork is human created.

Without A Net | G. O. Clark
G. O. Clark's work has been published in Asimov's, Analog, The Heartbeat Of The Universe Anthology, BFS Horizons (GB), and many others since last century. He is the author of 17 poetry collections, and 3 short story collections. He won the Asimov's Readers Award for poetry in 2001 & 2023, and was Stoker Award Poetry finalist in 2011. http://goclarkpoet.weebly.com

Uttered Awry | Scott J. Couturier
Scott J. Couturier is a Rhysling-nominated poet and prose writer of the weird, liminal, and darkly fantastic. His work has appeared in numerous venues, including The Audient Void, Spectral Realms, Space and Time Magazine, Cosmic Horror Monthly, Weirdbook, & Eternal Haunted Summer. His most recent publication is a collection of weird horror verse, Nightmuse: Poems of Speculative Darkness, released by Jackanapes Press in 2025. Couturier lives an obscure reverie in the wilds of northern Michigan with his partner/live-in editor and two cats.

popular | Lorraine Schein

Lorraine Schein is a NY writer. Her work has appeared in Strange Horizons, Scientific American, The Fairy Tale Magazine, the journal of the British Fantasy Society Horizons, and in the anthologies Underland Arcana and Tragedy Queens: Stories Inspired by Lana del Rey & Sylvia Plath. The Futurist's Mistress (poetry), is available from Mayapple Press. Her book of poems and stories, The Lady Anarchist Cafe, is available from Autonomedia and on Amazon. https://autonomedia.org/product/the-lady-anarchist-cafe/

An Eye In Time | Charlotte Holloway Ashwanden

They used to say to tell a story is to weave a magic spell; I'm not so sure they weren't right... I am a mother of two and live in the mountains in southern Spain, surrounded by magic and beauty and translating this into readable form to help nourish the soul of the world. My biggest literary influence is Ursula K LeGuin; I also play with mythological and psychological themes based in part from my studies of Joseph Campbell and CG Jung, as well as my explorations into Peace, and Conflict Resolution.

Sitting down to eat | Greg Beatty

Greg Beatty lives in Bellingham, Washington. He writes everything from jokes about cows to essays on cooking disasters, and has more dog friends than human friends. He blogs about picture books at It's a Picture Book World (https://itsapicturebookworld.com/).

The Black Sky Is a Puzzle Box | Brian Richards

Brian Richards grew up in central Pennsylvania and uses his experiences from teaching, software design, and travel to color in the dark corners of his poetry and fiction. He spends his mornings with his cat, too many hours after that at a keyboard, and the best parts of his day with his wife.

Moons in Circular | Shawn Scott Smith

Shawn Scott Smith is a writer of a bunch of published poems and short stories. He lives in Asheville, NC, plays pinball, and likes to meet new people. All of his adventures are documented on his website at luckycreature.com and most social media spots @lucky-creature

Warrior Dream | Kelly Talbot

Kelly Talbot has edited books and other content for 20 years for Wiley, Macmillan, Oxford, Pearson Education, and other publishers. Kelly's writing has appeared in dozens of magazines and anthologies. He divides his time between Indianapolis, United States, and Timisoara, Romania.

untitled haiku | John R. Platt

John R. Platt is an environmental journalist, poet, and artist. He is the editor of The Revelator, an environmental news and commentary site. Platt lives on the outskirts of Portland, Oregon, where he is surrounded by backyard chickens and cartoonists. https://linktr.ee/johnrplatt

Only Birds & Dreams | Nico Martinez Nocito
Nico Martinez Nocito (they/them) writes speculative fiction and poetry with a queer, feminist bent. Their work has been nominated for the Rhysling Award and published in Strange Horizons, Heartlines Spec, and Apex Magazine. Learn more about Nico and their writing on Bluesky and Instagram @nicowritesbooks, or on their website, nicoma rtineznocito.com.

ode to green stars | Lee Clark Zumpe
Lee Clark Zumpe, an entertainment editor with Tampa Bay Newspapers, earned his degree in English at the University of South Florida. He began writing poetry and fiction in the early 1990s. His work has appeared in a variety of literary journals, genre magazines, and anthologies. Recent publication credits include Spectral Realms, Dreams & Nightmares, and The Literary Hatchet. Lee lives on the west coast of Florida with his wife and daughter.

The Most Fateful Day in Earth History: Super Bowl CXLVIII, Sunday, February 4, 2114 | J. J. Steinfeld
Canadian poet, fiction writer, and playwright J. J. Steinfeld lives on Prince Edward Island, where he is patiently waiting for Godot's arrival and a phone call from Kafka. While waiting, he has published 25 books, including An Unauthorized Biography of Being (Stories, Ekstasis Editions, 2016), Absurdity, Woe Is Me, Glory Be (Poetry, Guernica Editions, 2017), A Visit to the Kafka Café (Poetry, Ekstasis Editions, 2018), Gregor Samsa Was Never in The Beatles (Stories, Ekstasis Editions, 2019), Morning Bafflement and Timeless Puzzlement (Poetry, Ekstasis Editions, 2020), Somewhat Absurd, Somehow Existential (Poetry, Guernica Editions, 2021), Acting on the Island (Stories, Pottersfield Press, 2022), As You Continue to Wait (Poetry, Ekstasis Editions, 2022), and My Post-Holocaust Second Generation Voice: History / Memory / Identity (Poetry, Ekstasis Editions, 2025); over 60 of his one-act plays and a handful of full-length plays have been performed in Canada and the United States, including the full-length plays The Franz Kafka Therapy Session, The Golden Age of Monsters, and A Television-Watching Artist; the one-act plays Godot's Leafless Tree, The Waiting Ends, The Entrance-or-Not Barroom, Freesias in Whiskey, Back to Back, No End in Sight, Flowers for the Vases, Sea Monsters, More Than Money, Imaginative Drinking, A Play of Disbelief, Memory Sounds, and In a Washroom of a Prestigious Art Gallery; and the audio plays In Becky's Name, A New Map, The Professor's Ashes, Diogenes' Lantern, and Laugh for Sanity.

Better | Pixie Bruner
Pixie Bruner (SFPA/DWS) is a writer, editor, and cancer survivor. She lives in Atlanta, GA, with her doppelgänger and deranged cats Her words are in the Elgin-nominated The Body As Haunted (Authortunities Press, 2024), Space & Time Magazine, Amazing Stories, Star*Line, Weird Fiction Quarterly, Abyss & Apex, Baubles from Bones, Strange Horizons, Angry Gable Press, and many more. She wrote for White Wolf Gaming Studio. Werespiders ruining LARPs were are her fault and was 2025 Rhysling Award Chair Survivor/2025 Kay Snow Prize Winner.

Second Sun | Brittany Redd
Brittany Redd is a teacher and writer whose poetry and fiction has been published in various literary magazines and anthologies and has been nominated for Best of the Net 2026. When not teaching or writing, she can be found traveling or hoarding polyhedral dice.

The Driven Snow | Lisa Timpf
Lisa Timpf is a retired HR and communications professional whose poetry has appeared in Eye to the Telescope, Star*Line, Triangulation: Seven-Day Weekend, and other venues. Lisa's speculative poetry collection Cats and Dogs in Space is available from Hiraeth Publishing. You can find out more about Lisa's writing projects at http://lisatimpf.bl ogspot.com/.

When Daylight Saving Ends | Wing Yau
Wing Yau is a Hong Kong–born poet whose recent work appears or is forthcoming in Dark Poets Club: Poetry Magazine, Lothlorien Poetry Journal, and Brushstrokes VI (2025). Their debut poetry collection, The Fiction of Flying, is forthcoming in 2026.

Men of the West Burn | Austin Schwartz
Hello, my name is Austin Schwartz, and my greatest inspiration is LOTR. When I first read *The Hobbit*, I finished it in less than 24 hours. I usually write in my free time or whenever inspiration hits me. My Dad owns a sailboat, which he half raised me on & I enjoy spending time in Nature to connect with God. I hope you have a wonderful day & God bless.

Sponsors of This Issue

Space & Time believes that great creative work deserves to be supported with the same care and intention with which it is made. Rather than filling our pages with traditional advertisements, we've chosen to feature a small number of aligned partners whose work we feel genuinely serves our readers.

Each sponsor in this section has been selected for their relevance to writers, creators, and storytellers. These are tools, books, services, and opportunities that contribute meaningfully to the creative ecosystem we're building together.

To preserve the reading experience, all sponsor features are gathered here, offering a dedicated space for discovery without interrupting the flow of the stories themselves.

Each feature includes a visual introduction to the work, a short editorial-style write-up curated by our team and simple way to learn more. In addition to appearing in the magazine, our sponsors are also mentioned on our weekly podcast and shared across our social media channels. This integrated approach allows us to highlight our sponsors across multiple touchpoints while maintaining a respectful experience for our readers.

If you're interested in being featured in an upcoming issue, we invite you to reach out. We're especially interested in partnering with creators, educators, publishers, and platforms that support the craft and business of writing. Details at the end of our sponsor section.

Thank you for supporting the work that supports writers.

— *Space & Time*

Everything Endless

by Linda D. Addison & Jamal Hodge

A luminous collaboration between Science Fiction & Fantasy Association Grand Master Linda D. Addison and visionary poet Jamal Hodge, *Everything Endless* explores the vastness of existence through a deeply human lens.

Moving between the cosmic and the intimate, this collection traces the story of life itself from creation, destruction, and the spaces in between while holding fast to a sense of hope rooted in imagination and creative possibility. Structured as a conversation, the poets alternate voices, weaving together distinct styles into a dynamic call-and-response that echoes across the page.

Grounded in both tradition and innovation, Addison and Hodge bring rhythm, precision, and emotional depth to each piece. Their work carries the energy of performance and the clarity of vision, balancing scientific wonder with lyrical intensity.

Praised for its "gorgeous blend of science fiction and lyrical poetry" (Sheree Renée Thomas) and described as capturing "the depth, complexity, beauty, and terror of dark poetry" (Jonathan Maberry), *Everything Endless* offers a powerful meditation on the universe—and our place within it.

Learn more: rawdogscreaming.com/book/everything-endless

Silk & Sinew: A Collection of Folk Horror from the Asian Diaspora

edited by Kristy Park Kulski

Named by the New York Public Library as one of the best new horror books of 2025, *Silk & Sinew* is a striking anthology that weaves together voices from across the Asian diaspora into a rich and unsettling tapestry of folk horror.

Rooted in the body with muscle, bone, sinew, these stories and poems explore how culture, memory, and identity manifest through physical and ancestral experience. The result is a collection that feels both intimate and expansive, drawing on tradition while reshaping the boundaries of the genre.

Edited by Bram Stoker Award–nominee Kristy Park Kulski, the anthology features an impressive lineup of contributors, including Ai Jiang, Nadia Bulkin, Christina Sng, Rena Mason, Lee Murray, J.A.W. McCarthy, Geneve Flynn, Bryan Thao Worra, and many more, with a foreword by Monika Kim.

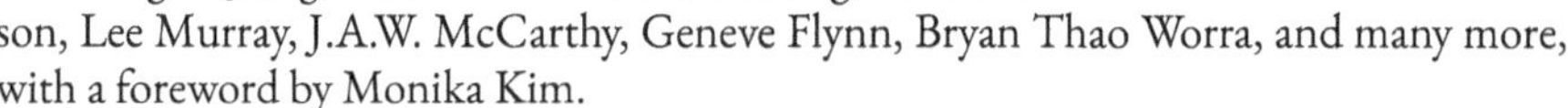

Praised as "a triumph of an anthology and an essential addition to the folk horror genre" (Eliza Chan) and "one of those rare books destined to become future literary classics" (Nuzo Onoh), *Silk & Sinew* stands as both a celebration of diasporic storytelling and a powerful evolution of modern horror.

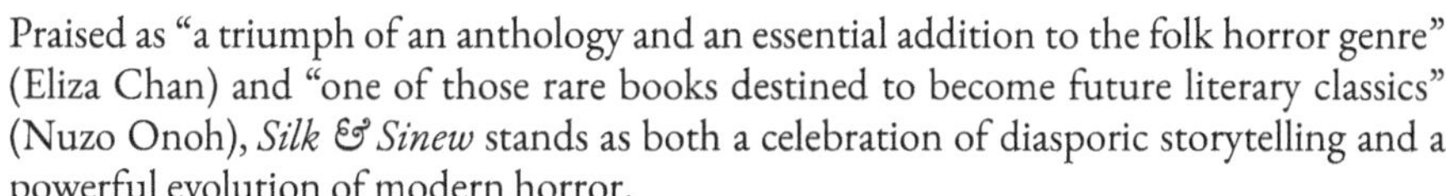

Learn more: garnetonwinter.com

A Fragile Thing

by Stephanie Ellis

Set against the shadowed streets and drawing rooms of Victorian London, *A Fragile Thing* follows Isaac Bercow as a man driven by ambition, curiosity, and a desire to be believed. With little to lose and everything to prove, Isaac pursues recognition for his abilities in mesmerism, seeking influence in a society where science and spiritualism entwine in equal measure.

What begins as a pursuit of validation soon deepens into something far more dangerous. As Isaac navigates a world of performance, persuasion, and power, he becomes entangled in deception and increasingly perilous alliances. The line between control and manipulation begins to blur, raising unsettling questions about agency, identity, and the limits of the human mind.

Rooted in gothic atmosphere and psychological tension, the novel explores the fragility of perception and how easily it can be shaped, distorted, or broken. As Lee Murray notes, Ellis delivers "a darkly chilling novel of madness, mind games, and manipulation... blurring the lines between illusion and reality," while Catherine McCarthy describes it as "oozing with Victorian Gothic," a story that leaves readers questioning who is monster and who is man.

Learn more: watertowerhill.com/stephanieellis

HorrorAddicts.net

created by Emerian Rich

Born from a passion for all things that haunt, unsettle, and inspire, *HorrorAddicts.net* is a living, breathing ecosystem for horror lovers. Founded in 2008, this multifaceted platform blends podcast, blog, and publishing house into a single immersive experience designed "for horror addicts, by horror addicts."

At its core, *HorrorAddicts.net* champions creators. Through interviews, reviews, fiction, and curated features, it amplifies the voices of writers, musicians, artists, and storytellers across the genre, creating a space where emerging talent and seasoned professionals coexist in a shared celebration of the dark.

Whether through its long-running podcast, themed digital magazines like *Horror Curated*, or its steady stream of articles and anthologies, the platform invites readers to engage with horror in all its forms, from the intimate to the expansive.

Rooted in community and creative exploration, *HorrorAddicts.net* thrives on diversity of voice and vision. Its content ranges from flash fiction to in-depth essays, from eerie folklore to experimental dark fantasy, weaving together a tapestry that reflects the many facets of fear, fascination, and imagination.

The result is a dynamic hub that feels both curated and communal as a place where horror is not merely consumed, but created, discussed, and lived. For readers, listeners, and creators alike, *HorrorAddicts.net* stands as a testament to the enduring power of the genre and the vibrant community that continues to shape its future.

Learn more: horroraddicts.net

Partner With Space & Time

We invite aligned creators, educators, publishers, and platforms to support the creative ecosystem alongside us.

We are currently offering a limited number of sponsor placements per issue (typically 4–5), ensuring that each feature receives focused attention rather than competing for visibility.

Our introductory rate for May is $100 per placement. This is a special launch rate as we develop and refine this program. Future issues may reflect updated pricing as our reach and offerings continue to grow.

Please email angelayurikosmith@gmail.com with the subject line:
May Sponsor Inquiry for Space & Time

Include the following:

- A brief description of your book, product, or service
- A high-resolution image (book cover, product image, or logo)
- A link you'd like readers to visit (website or landing page preferred)

To ensure compatibility across all distribution platforms, we direct readers to sponsor websites or landing pages rather than retail storefronts.

All sponsor features are editorially curated and written in-house to maintain tone and consistency. **Due to limited placements, not all submissions will be accepted.**

www.ingramcontent.com/pod-product-compliance
Lightning Source LLC
LaVergne TN
LVHW020656100826
845148LV00012B/2525

* 9 7 9 8 9 0 2 2 8 0 0 4 0 *